The Wishing Window Well

The Wishing Window Well

Aubrey Fogle

Pleasant Word
A Division of WinePress Group

Pleasant Word (a division of WinePress Publishing, PO Box 428, Enumclaw, WA 98022) functions only as a book publisher. As such, the ultimate design, content, editorial accuracy, and views expressed or implied in this work are those of the author.

ISBN 13: 978-1-4141-1590-0
ISBN 10: 1-4141-1590-3
Library of Congress Catalog Card Number: 2009909160

To Dad who, by example, sparked my
love for writing in the first place, and

To Mom, who kindled that spark
every step along the way.

Contents

Chapter 1

No Pets Allowed

NO PETS ALLOWED. If Allison Sutton could choose three words to sum up her entire twelve-year-old life, they would be *no pets allowed*. Though her entire life consisted of only twelve years, they had been twelve long ones—twelve long years without a pet. To remember a time when she had not longed for a pet was like asking her to remember a time when she had not liked mashed potatoes.

But the closest she'd ever gotten to fulfilling her pet dreams was a goldfish. Frail, the goldfish, who was never hardy to begin with (and so was appropriately named), lasted only six hours from the time he was deposited into the fishbowl to the time he was deposited into the toilet bowl. And one of the six hours did not even count, because the last hour consisted of a feebly floating Frail, who remained noncommittal as to whether he was dead or alive, at the top of the bowl full of water. There he drifted until he was pronounced dead by Annie Sutton, who, at two years of age, thought she knew everything. Quite the energetic argument ensued among the Sutton children as to whether Frail had indeed "breathed his last," a phrase that Allison, the eldest of the Sutton children, enjoyed using whenever the opportunity arose, which, as she discovered, was rare.

Finally Teresa, who was seven, asked, "How can we tell if Frail has breathed his last?"

"Goldfish do not breathe in the sense that we do," reasoned Bessie, the second eldest, who was extremely rational. "That is, they do not breathe out of their mouths."

While some of the younger Suttons somberly reflected on this thought, Allison, who loved to use new dramatic expressions, was disappointed with Bessie for ruining her well-timed phrase of "breathed his last."

Bessie, a peacemaker, and not ever having intended to provoke her older sister, asked, "So do you think Frail has breathed his last in the fish way of doing it?" She squinted at Frail, with her glasses riding up on her freckled nose.

Not overly eager to pass the death sentence, Allison sighed. "There is always hope. Let's wait a little bit longer."

And so they did. Thirty seconds of dead silence ensued and was finally broken by Allison, who, compelled by her duty as the eldest child, sought to kindle hope in the ever doubtful-looking situation.

"I remember once in second grade when Leonard Ball had to flush his goldfish down the toilet. It was flushed prematurely and returned the next day in the toilet bowl . . . alive!"

An awed hush fell over the children as they contemplated this miraculous return. No one questioned its authenticity. Still reluctant to declare a final verdict, the children called upon their mother to confirm their growing suspicion that Frail had indeed breathed his last.

Mrs. Sutton came in with Baron, the youngest of the Sutton children, strapped onto her back, and paused in front of the fishbowl. Baron, sensing excitement building, stiffened his arms and let out a squeal directly into his mother's left ear. Startled at the volume of the scream, she cut short her examination of the fish.

Grimacing, Mrs. Sutton said apologetically, "Yes, I'm afraid there's no more life in Frail."

The children knew they had hoped against hope. Their sinking hearts at the sobering news bore evidence of this. The time had come to say their good-byes, and with a flush they said farewell to Frail.

So ended the trauma of the first pet. Such an experience hardly counted as having a pet, the Sutton children reasoned. But whether it counted or not held little import to Mrs. Sutton, who was the chief reason why their childhoods were deprived of the Lassies and Black Beauties of the world.

While Dr. Sutton had a similar love of pets as his children and sympathized with them accordingly, he valued his wife's happiness above his children's. So it seemed that Allison's hope of ever having a pet had been flushed away with Frail.

". . . and *no pets allowed*," concluded Dr. Sutton. "That's what our landlord says here in our rental agreement." He closed the folder marked "Rental House" and set it down on the kitchen table.

"Seems like a good fit," commented Mrs. Sutton as she finished feeding Baron.

"Why do you think there are no pets allowed? It is in the country, right?" asked Allison, sounding disappointed.

Baron started wailing, to which Mrs. Sutton responded with a set of vigorous thumps on his back in the hopes of ridding his system of gas bubbles. After four hearty whacks, Baron gave a tremendous burp and ceased his fussing, which produced proud applause from two of the middle Sutton children, Teresa and Josiah.

Thankful for the quiet, Allison again asked her father why the owner had said no pets were allowed.

"Probably for the same reason we have the exact rule," said Mrs. Sutton, dabbing at a spot of spit-up on her shoulder. (This too brought forth applause from the same two middle Sutton children.)

Disappointment rose within Allison, because she had asked her father, who, she had hoped, would have shared some sympathy for her—the real motive behind her question.

Sensing Allison's sad gaze still upon her, Mrs. Sutton added the one well-familiar phrase of hope she ever offered: "When you have your own house, you can have all the animals you want."

Allison was never fully consoled by this consideration.

"And when you become a mom, you can drink pop any time you want to. Right, Mom?" asked Teresa, grabbing Mrs. Sutton's Diet Coke can. Giving one of her silly smiles, she posed as if someone were taking a picture of her.

Mrs. Sutton affirmed absentmindedly that when you are a mom you can have all the pets and pop you want.

"I can't wait to be a mommy!" cried Teresa. And then, as if a whole new world had just opened before her, she declared, "I can't wait to be a mommy, because then I can do whatever I want!" In the midst of this last epiphany, she began running around wildly, waving her hands in a most frenzied manner.

But Teresa's last outcry was ignored, because Annie was yelling from the bathroom that she needed help washing her hands, and Josiah spilled his grape juice across the entire length of the kitchen table. The traveling purple liquid seeped through the two major leaf cracks of the table and pooled in the lap of Mrs. Sutton, who had just finished wiping away Baron's latest spit-up from her shoulder.

"Haven't I asked you to put a lid on your cup when you have grape juice?" she asked, trying to remain calm as she caught the remaining drips with Baron's burp rag.

As Josiah darted for the tissue box, he cried that he was sorry. He whipped out the tissues and frantically threw wads of them onto Mrs. Sutton's lap before she had a chance to object. Having absorbed the juice within moments, the flimsy tissues simply dissolved into clumps of soggy tissue.

Dr. Sutton and Bessie, the helpful child of the family, quickly came to the rescue, Bessie taking the baby from Mrs. Sutton and Dr. Sutton grabbing substantial rags to take care of the mess that Josiah had only since multiplied.

At the beginning of the chaos, Allison had conveniently remembered something that required her immediate attention somewhere in a part of the house that was within safe calling distance. This habit of disappearing when the opportunity for service arose was attributed to Allison's weak work ethic, as Dr. Sutton would say. Once she entered her own quiet room, she plopped down on her bed and lazily reached for the worn library book that lay open on her bedside table.

Feeling sorry for herself, she sighed and longingly flipped through the pages. There was no page that she was not familiar with; in fact, she was sure she had memorized all the breeds. Last month she had familiarized herself with the horse breeds, and now she had finished the breeds of dogs. Sitting on her bed, she looked out her window—as was one of her favorite habits—at the stars and wished, hoped, and prayed that someday, one day soon, she could have a pet of her own. She had thought that with moving from the suburbs of Chicago and out to the country, she would finally have her chance at having a pet. Closing her pale blue eyes, she fell back onto her pillow. Words, awful words, ran through her head. Her father's voice, haunting, echoed in her mind: *"No pets allowed."*

Chapter 2

The Window Well

WITHIN A MONTH, the Sutton family found themselves weaving and bumping their way down a winding, country, gravel road towards their new home. A quaint, grayish-blue house finally greeted them at the end of a long, rocky driveway. The car had barely come to a halt before the four oldest Sutton children were already sprinting toward the front door. Giddy with excitement, they bounced on the porch as they waited for Dr. Sutton to come and unlock the door.

"Now remember," Dr. Sutton said as his feet crunched over the gravel, "Allison and Bessie, you will share the bedroom to the right of the bathroom. And Teresa and Josiah, yours will be the bedroom to the left."

Allison smiled at Bessie, and Teresa smiled at Josiah, and suddenly they were thankful that they had all decided long ago to be friends. It made life a lot easier.

As the door was finally opened, Allison spotted a deer gracefully lunging over the fence that ran alongside their driveway. She stood still a moment as her heart raced at the wonder of having such beautiful creatures in her own new yard. The other children, having missed the sight, had long since disappeared into the basement.

Abruptly, a horrible thought entered Allison's mind as she too began the descent into the basement. *What if the bedroom has no windows?* It was quite a dreadful thought. Looking out the window had been her routine, her nightly ritual. In it she found safety, security, and serenity.

Then with amazement she heard Bessie shouting delightfully, "Allison, you would not believe it! Guess what our bedroom has!"

Without guessing, Allison raced into the room she assumed would be theirs and looked around expectantly.

Bessie proudly walked over to one of the walls that lined the outside of the house and pointed.

Allison glimpsed to where Bessie pointed and inhaled sharply.

"Did you ever imagine it?" asked Bessie excitedly. Her grayish-blue eyes sparkled with merriment.

Allison's face neared the window well, and crinkles outlined the corners of her eyes as a smile slowly spread across her face.

"You will still be able to see the stars," Bessie whispered.

As Bessie stood there beaming, Allison couldn't help but be amazed at how Bessie always got joy out of someone else's happiness. She could count on one hand the number of times she had seen Bessie not happy.

"Would you mind if I have my bed on this side of the wall?" Allison asked, indicating the wall that contained the window well. "And your bunk bed could go on the opposite side."

As Bessie nodded, Dr. Sutton poked his head inside their room. "Everything okay in here?" he asked.

"We have a window in our bedroom after all!" exclaimed Allison, still looking up at the sky through the windowpane, which was speckled with dried mud.

"That's good," said Dr. Sutton, a bit distracted. "I'll need you guys to stay out of the way when the movers start bringing things down here."

For ten minutes Allison and Bessie talked about how they wanted their room set up. Then the movers came. Mrs. Sutton was the final authority on how the furniture was to be arranged. Once in the girls' bedroom, she ushered Bessie aside to make room for the movers, who were bringing in her bunk bed.

"My bunk bed goes over here," Bessie said with an air of authority, "and Allison's bed goes right under the window."

"What window?" asked the muffled voice of one of the movers, whose head was hidden behind a mattress.

"The window well," corrected Mrs. Sutton.

Allison hustled out of the way, while thinking of the name of the window. It seemed to fit its description perfectly—*a window sunk below ground, yet opened to the sky above . . . just like a well.*

Just then, from somewhere upstairs Dr. Sutton called down to the two eldest girls. Leaving her new bedroom in a dream-like fashion, Allison rolled the words with her tongue: *window well.*

Chapter 3

A Boy with a Tail

THE MONTHS FOLLOWING their move passed by unusually fast, as the children had a new house and a new yard to explore. Having moved during summer instead of the school year, the Suttons had not met many children. Nor did they meet any of the neighborhood children, as there was no neighborhood. Rather, every fourth mile or so another gravel driveway, like their own, would spout down through a valley or disappear into a thick wood. The children could only guess that there lay a house at the end. But this shortage of neighbors turned out to bond the children even closer together than they had been before.

The Hill family, who had been friends from their old neighborhood, came to visit them over Labor Day weekend. Three children exactly the same ages of the three oldest Sutton children had been, in Allison's own words, the "constant companions of our youth." While they had been friends in the "city," they found their friendships deepen even more now that they were in the country. Exploration hikes, campfires, walks, tree climbing, swimming, and carving things in dead tree trunks were all part of the weekend.

Toward the end of their visit, knowing that their time left at the Suttons' was short, Daniel, who was Allison's age and always eager to squeeze in the most fun as possible, suggested that they play Sardines. Everyone agreed.

Still in their swimsuits, they began an exciting game. First Bessie hid (because Allison had suggested it), while the rest of the children counted, but she was found quickly under the porch steps. Teresa, having been the last to find Bessie, hid next. She too was found quickly by everyone except Daniel, who immediately confessed he had done it on purpose because he wanted to be the next one to hide.

"Nobody will find me," he announced, waving his hands and hopping from one foot to another.

This statement of course egged on the other children's resolve to find him even faster than they had found Bessie or Teresa. And so, with haste they began counting with all eagerness to prove Daniel wrong.

As usual, Teresa and Wendy, being the same age, stuck together in their search for Daniel. Both had wild, curly hair that was never kept in line. Brightly colored t-shirts hung loose around their sinewy bodies and in no way matched the skirts they wore. Every day they wore skirts that Wendy's grandma, who was well versed in the girls' wide range of interests, had made especially for them. The many yards of fabric afforded excellent means for spinning, and at the left side of each waist was sewn a special loophole for their pocket knives.

Teresa and Wendy were the only two who had not gone swimming, because they had been in the middle of serving to their dolls a delectable feast consisting entirely of beads. Brilliantly colored beads in small, quaint dishes had been carefully prepared for hours over the entire span of the weekend. Blueberry pies, savory soups, and steaming casseroles were just a few among the myriads of dishes they had prepared. Needless to say, they were too engrossed in their cookery to be concerned about swimming. And it was only at the persuasion of both their mothers that they left their luscious spread and got some fresh air.

So Teresa and Wendy went one direction, skirts flapping in the wind, while Bessie and Abbey went another. Allison was left on her own, for she usually stuck with Daniel, whom she determined to be the first to find. And find him she did. This was no surprise, for they thought a lot alike.

Teresa and Wendy were too close at hand when she thought she spied Daniel's bleach-colored hair sticking slightly above the window well.

"I wonder where he is!" Allison said loud enough for the girls to hear as she raced off in the opposite direction of the window well. Then with a pounding heart, she hurried back to the window well as soon as the slight figures of Teresa and Wendy disappeared around the house.

Extremely satisfied with herself for having found him first and without anyone else's knowledge, she scrunched down beside him, almost weak with giddiness.

It was a tight fit, and with Daniel's elbow driving ever more heavily into her back, she began to wish that the others had seen her slip into the window well.

Thankfully, the next to discover them were Teresa and Wendy. Everyone positioned themselves in what was initially an agreeable arrangement. Unfortunately, it was only agreeable for so long. Pretty soon, Allison began wishing that Teresa and Wendy came with a little more cushioning around their bones.

They all held their breath as Bessie and Abbey came dangerously close to the window well.

"Looks like Teresa and Wendy are gone too," said Abbey nonchalantly.

"Yeah," returned Bessie without much concern.

The four children in the window well exchanged gleeful glances, and soon they breathed easily again as their sisters ambled away.

As Allison began to weary of looking at the same spider web, Daniel began to fidget.

Allison put her finger to her lips. *"Shhh!"*

He stilled for a moment, only to resume his squirming seconds later with renewed vigor.

"Dan!" Wendy said.

But Daniel was not to be shushed. Allison, being a keen observer, noticed Daniel's eyes widen with terror.

Fear of the unknown gripped Allison as she whispered, "What's wrong?"

She received her answer, but not in the usual fashion. Never before had anyone shot out of the window well as did Daniel that day. Or so it appeared to Bessie and Abbey, who stood a short distance away. To their utter marvel and astonishment, what they saw led them to believe Daniel had indeed sprung forth from the ground below. But this was not the only cause of amazement; he had emerged with a tail. A long, black tail about half of Daniel's length swayed nimbly to and fro as any tail would be expected to do. Daniel, with his latest attachment, flew wildly about, screeching in a most terrible manner.

"What is he doing?" Bessie asked as they laughed at Daniel, who was known to be an entertainer.

But the remaining three, left stunned in the window well, did not think to laugh. Their mouths had gone dry, and their limbs went helplessly limp. The close-up view afforded them the truth of the matter. Daniel had not grown a tail, nor was he trying to be funny. The long, black tail was a snake that had perceptively fixed its mouth precisely where one would expect a tail to grow.

Teresa, Wendy, and Allison tore out of the window well and fled into the house, babbling some nonsense that their parents had difficulty deciphering. Words such as "Daniel," "bottom," and "snake" were no sooner flung at them as they were outside of the house, rushing to help Daniel, who had by now run some distance from the window well, yet still flew about in a most frantic, frenzied manner.

The hysterical cries from both mothers did nothing save to add to Daniel's panic.

"Do something, Allen!" screamed Mrs. Sutton at Dr. Sutton as she wrung her hands.

Either the fathers' calm fed the fire of the mothers' hysteria or the hysteria fed the fire of the calm. No one could tell who was feeding which fire. But one thing was clear: the more hysterical the mothers became, the calmer the fathers grew. All the rest of the children remained at a safe distance away.

It was amazing to watch their fathers at work. Pride welled up within the hearts of the children as they watched the collectedness of thought and swiftness of movement of both fathers as they, without so much as a word, neared Daniel. It was as if each father had read the other's mind, for there was no need for discussion.

Their first goal was to calm Daniel down, which they soon realized Daniel would not do on his own. When the mothers realized that a snake had lodged itself securely into Daniel's rear, they began screaming louder than Daniel, which complicated matters even more.

Simultaneously, Dr. Sutton and Mr. Hill rushed at Daniel and in one fell swoop managed to pin him to the ground. A stressed but thankful half-sigh, half-scream came forth from the mothers as they too rushed to the scene. With sympathetic amazement, the other children crept behind the mothers more cautiously. The only noises that came from Daniel's mouth were smothered whimpers, because his face was hidden in the grass.

Both mothers kept shouting the obvious.

"It's attached!" Daniel's mother cried.

"Help him," Mrs. Sutton said.

"I am so sorry," Mrs. Sutton said over and over again to Daniel's mother.

These declarations only stirred up Daniel's moans.

"Daniel, you need to hold still," his father said, "if we are going to be able to help you."

"Is it still on me?" Daniel sobbed, not trusting his nerves to look.

"Yes, it is still on you. Don't you feel it?" replied his father, somewhat confused.

Dr. Sutton, surprised by Daniel's question, suddenly realized that there was no blood in sight. By this time, Daniel lay sprawled out flat on his stomach, while around his rear gathered both sets of parents. The black snake continued to wriggle violently.

Upon closer inspection, at which point the rest of the children graciously looked away, Daniel's dad stated in a relieved voice, "I think it's stuck on Daniel's swim trunks."

After the quick but thorough examination, the dads made the accurate assessment that the snake was attached to Daniel, not by a bite that had penetrated the skin, but by its fangs being caught in the mesh lining of Daniel's swimsuit. Nothing short of the complete removal of the swim trunks would be necessary. Without anything needing to be said, the children turned about and raced into the house, where they were left to review and discuss the most unusual occurrence that had just transpired.

Moments later, the mothers brought Daniel, looking haggard and exhausted, into the house.

Soft, concerned questions such as, "Are you okay?" were whispered in his direction.

A quiet hush that never left until after their company had departed fell over the rest of the children.

It was a good thing the Hill family was scheduled to leave because, despite varying and numerous efforts, Daniel's good humor was never restored.

Later that evening, as Allison lay in her bed looking up through her window well, she reflected on the fact that the snake had happened to get into the window well.

"Bess?" Allison asked hesitantly, as neither girl had spoken for ten minutes. "Are you still awake?"

"Yeah," Bessie murmured.

"If a snake was in the window well, do you think we might find something else in there some day?"

"Maybe."

"Maybe it will be something different next time."

Allison did not pursue further conversation, and as her thoughts drifted to sleep, she dreamily wondered when something else might someday find itself in her window well.

Chapter 4

Fishing for Mice

THE HOPE OF finding something else in the window well soon faded, as most things do, with time. Piles of leaves soon disappeared under layers of snow, and once again hats, mittens, scarves, heavy coats, and snow pants were pulled out of their various storage bins. No matter how organized Mrs. Sutton tried to be, the inevitable yearly discovery would be made that all items that had fit last year (though even this was questionable) certainly would not fit this year. Although Mrs. Sutton expected this, it was nonetheless a trying experience.

Winter clothing was not the only troubling aspect of winter. Along with winter came mice. No part of the house, or so it seemed, was left unspoiled by them. Mice had left their droppings in cupboards, chewed through shirts in the laundry baskets, and had actually been spotted in the bathtub. None of the five human senses were exempt; that year in the rental house the mice were experienced in their entirety. The ears of all members of the Sutton household heard the sounds of their faint scamperings inside multiple walls and ceilings at all times of the day. The eyes of various members of the household spied the mice as they whisked their small bodies out of sight through disturbingly small spaces. The noses of all family members smelled the occasional stench of decaying mice remnants located somewhere under the staircase, although the precise location was not known. The sensation of touch was claimed by Josiah, who, though at four years of age, had vowed that his sleep had been interrupted by a tickling underneath his nose. This impression had been later pronounced a mouse. Josiah was not known for lying. The final and fifth sense of taste went to Baron. At nine months, anything and everything that his chubby hands laid hold of went directly into his mouth. One morning, Bessie, who happened to be passing through the living room where Baron was happily playing, noticed him intensely concentrating on sampling some mysterious object in his mouth. Upon examination (a finger fishing inside the slobbery mouth), it was found to be a mouse dropping. This event was immediately recorded in Baron's baby book by Bessie, to whom Mrs. Sutton had designated the task.

One night, after the usual ritual of staring out the window well, dreamily imagining how life would be with a pet, Allison snuggled down deep into her covers. Just as Allison's and Bessie's heavy eyelids had finally shut in sleep, the well-known scratchy scamper of a mouse graced their ears. The girls' eyes remained shut tightly, as if the force with which they closed them would have any effect on whether the scuttles and scurries of the mouse would cease. But they continued, and then each girl slowly opened her eyes.

"If it doesn't stop soon, *someone* should go get Dad," Allison said.

Now, all they had to do was wait. But after they waited in silence for a minute, Allison said in a groggy whisper, "I don't think it is going to stop."

Bessie responded by groping for her glasses and fumbling out the door. Feeling a little sense of guilt at not having gone herself, Allison snuggled more deeply into her covers and waited for the report. But there wasn't much of one.

Waiting until she had situated herself back into her bed, Bessie announced, "Dad didn't really say anything."

With neither of them being exactly satisfied, they settled back down, this time more awake than ever. It took much longer now to become tired again, and just as they both were getting sleepy, the noise started up once more.

All attempts to ignore the noises were impossible. As time went on, the sounds increasingly became confined to one area—directly above Allison's headboard. Exasperated, Allison sat up. What she did next surprised even herself.

Whack! Thump! Smack! went Allison's hands against her side of the bedroom wall.

Arms suspended in the air, she waited. The pattering within the ceiling went directly over Bessie's bunk bed. Never had she been so thankful that she always slept on the bottom bunk, while the top bunk remained vacant. The sound halted precisely above the bunk.

Catching on, Bessie sat up and drummed on her wall. This again produced the desired effect, and the scraping of little mouse feet took off toward the way from which it had just come. Allison was ready for it. As soon as it halted somewhere above her, she wailed mightily, slapping and walloping the wall. The faint sounds that followed the girls' violent percussions on the wall were evidence of a disturbed and most confused mouse. Back to Bessie's wall it went. She too was in ready position. Both girls by now had a giddy gleam of delight spread across their faces. Bessie, for a second time, successfully sent the mouse back to Allison who, by this time, was laughing hysterically. So giddy was she that she didn't know how much strength she'd have this time to whack the wall. She never found out.

A huffing figure shadowed their doorway, crying, "What's wrong?!"

With withering hearts they realized it was their father.

"Oh, I am so sorry!" Allison offered weakly.

"It was just the mice," Bessie began.

Having ascertained that nothing was the matter, in a hurried tone Dr. Sutton said they'd talk about it in the morning, and abruptly left. The ensuing silence was never broken the rest of that night. It was as if the mouse too had been reprimanded, for they didn't hear it again.

It was not until after breakfast that Allison and Bessie offered their dad a humble explanation for what had taken place the night before. Dr. Sutton listened without a word, his left eye raised in a question. Feeling justified, the girls ran off to get ready for school. If they imagined their words had gone unheard, they were wrong. That night, Dr. Sutton laid down mousetrap after mousetrap in several strategic places throughout the basement ceiling. This was possible because the ceilings were suspended, a ceiling that was made of sections that could easily be lifted up by a mere nudge of the hand. So easily could the ceilings come up, that whenever Allison or Bessie would close their bedroom door suddenly, multiple panels of ceiling would flutter up and down like the keys of a programmed piano. It was these ceiling sections that Dr. Sutton lifted up and carefully placed the mouse traps behind.

"We'll see if this doesn't take care of the problem," he said as he carefully set another trap and then carefully put the ceiling panel back into place.

"Now there is no reason for anyone to lift up the panels while the traps are up there," he said, climbing off a chair.

Allison and Bessie nodded somberly, though inside their hearts they rejoiced that their pleas had been heeded. There was nothing left to do but wait. And they did not have to wait for long.

That night, as Allison and Bessie lay in their beds deep in sleep, they were suddenly awakened by a loud snap right above the empty top bunk bed. Bessie, in the bunk below, shivered.

"There is nothing like being awakened to the sound of death," commented Allison as she fought off a sad and eerie feeling.

Silently, Bessie pulled the covers up close to her nose. "Well, at least it's not dead right above your head," she said, not at all liking the thought that the mouse had died somewhere over her.

"But at least the top bunk provides an additional barrier between you and the deceased," Allison said encouragingly, thankful that it wasn't her.

After a while the girls once again settled down to sleep, but in vain. A scraping noise in the vicinity where the recent death had just occurred caused both girls to reopen their eyes in strange horror.

Bessie opened her mouth to say something, when Allison hushed her by putting a finger to her own mouth and then mouthed the word "wait." Their patience was soon rewarded by the same sound, only this time the scraping sounded stronger.

"It sounds like something is being scooted or scraped," whispered Bessie.

She had since left her bed and joined Allison in hers. The scooting noise, directly above her, even though still separated by the top bunk, was too unnerving—at least until they figured out what was causing the strange noise.

They listened again, and once more their ears were satisfied with the same noise.

"It is too strong of a sound for a mouse. It doesn't patter like a mouse. It couldn't be the mouse that just died," Allison said, unconvinced.

Again and again they heard the noise, and each time, the girls exchanging looks. Before long they concluded that the noise was traveling. With every scrape the disturbing noise grew louder and closer.

"It's making its way over here. It's traveling this way," Bessie said nervously.

The same sobering idea seemed to cross their minds simultaneously. Allison's bed, unlike Bessie's, did not have a top bunk to act as a barrier between them and "it."

"If it ends up over my bed, I'm getting in yours, because I don't want to sleep in the top bunk either," Allison said, fumbling for a pair of socks at the bottom of her bed. The plethora of dirty socks was the reason for the perpetual bulge at the end of the bed and the reason Bessie allowed her legs to go only so far in the recesses of her sister's bed.

"Next time we hear it, let's make a run for it," Allison said, having successfully found a pair that suited her.

Barely had she finished these words when they heard it again and, in response, fled to the opposite side of the room to Bessie's bed. The troubled girls, who by now were contemplating the idea of getting Dad, breathed heavily from their recent sprint.

"Are you thinking what I'm thinking?" Allison asked her sister, her eyebrows raised.

"It's your turn," Bessie said, initially glad to make the observation. But as she thought further she wasn't sure which would be worse—waking up their father or staying alone in their bedroom.

Having made up their minds that their situation was "Dad-worthy," Allison prepared to leave the room.

But Bessie, who had made up her mind quickly, had no desire to be left alone in the room with the unidentified scooting, scratching thing and quickly followed close at the heels of her older sister. Allison wasn't surprised.

"It still counts as my turn," Allison said to clarify.

Courage began to fail as they drew nearer to the bedroom of their sleeping parents. Through the open door they heard nothing but the steady sound of breathing. They hovered for what seemed like hours at the doorway, hoping their parents would miraculously sense their presence. Waking up one's parents was a dreadful deed. Suddenly, the noise didn't seem too big of a deal anymore, and having given each other the knowing "look," with all haste they retreated back to their bedroom. Neither girl spoke as they entered their bedroom again. Standing in the middle of the room, they waited to hear the dragging noise, to make sure they knew where it was. Having taken note of the general vicinity of the phantom mouse, which was by this time straight above Allison's single bed, the girls quickly sped toward the bunk beds, Bessie in her usual bottom bunk with Allison right by her side. They didn't know how long they listened to the noise that night, but soon they became too tired to care anymore and fell asleep.

They gave the night's report first thing in the morning, over a bowl of oatmeal. (Allison liked sprinkling brown sugar at both the bottom and the top of her bowl. She would never stir in the sugar but would eat the oatmeal all around it, so that the last few mouthfuls were almost pure sugar.) They didn't mention the failed expedition to their parents' room. Immediately after breakfast was cleared, Dr. Sutton and the rest of the Sutton family followed the girls eagerly down to their room. Everyone gathered in close. Allison didn't know why, but a special feeling came over her when her whole family was in her room.

"Why are you putting gloves on?" asked Josiah, watching intently as Dr. Sutton stretched the white medical gloves over his muscular hands.

"Mice are very dirty, and you don't want to touch them with your bare hands if you can help it," he said with a final snap of the gloves.

Teresa handed her father an empty grocery sack as he mounted the bunk bed steps to examine the place where he had laid the trap the previous night. Everyone held their breath with anticipation. The only noise they heard as Dr. Sutton slowly raised the ceiling panel was the squealing of Baron, who was excited by the intense silence. At first, when Dr. Sutton began to lift the panel, his head remained a good distance from his hands, which were courageously holding up the panel. Squinting, he slowly bent his head closer, while he raised the panel higher. His head looked as if it were inside the ceiling.

"Rarrrrrrrr!" wailed Josiah, more loudly than what even exceeded the proper level for outdoor voices.

Needless to say, if there had ever been a perfect moment for such a scare, this would have been it.

Mrs. Sutton and the rest of the children screamed and started in fright, and had it not been for their father, would have laughed good-naturedly afterward. Dr. Sutton, perched precariously on the bunk-bed stairs, jerked backward and just barely regained his balance. It was a good thing that no further injury had been done to Dr. Sutton, for even still, Josiah received censure of the gravest kind. But it had been worth it.

And so the whole process began all over again, with Dr. Sutton examining and the rest of the family watching.

"Be careful, honey," Mrs. Sutton said.

"The trap is . . . gone," observed Dr. Sutton.

Feeling justified, Allison and Bessie smiled triumphantly at each other.

"Where did you hear the scooting noise?" asked Dr. Sutton as he climbed down the ladder.

"Right above my bed," Allison replied, pointing to the area.

As a group, the whole family shuffled toward Allison's bed. Dr. Sutton stepped on top of Allison's bed, from which Allison had promptly removed her pillow. For the third time the whole process was repeated, but this time with different results.

In doctor-like fashion, Dr. Sutton began a careful procedure of removing what the rest of the family guessed was the trap. No one asked him any questions as he went about his business, which was just the way they knew he liked it. ("Questions at such a time like this reflect more a lack of patience than a desire for instruction," he often said.)

To the satisfaction of all, Dr. Sutton drew forth a trap with a dead mouse. He then deposited it distastefully into the grocery sack, which Teresa had been holding open in eager anticipation.

Climbing down from the bed, Dr. Sutton took the sack from Teresa, tied it up, and handed it to Josiah, who, for some reason, was anxious to hold it.

"So it must have made its way over there before it died?" Mrs. Sutton asked.

"It lasted long enough to drag itself all the way across the ceiling. Must be the hardy country mouse," said Dr. Sutton, looking upward.

"It suffered a long, painful death," Allison mused.

Their contemplation was interrupted by an outburst of anger from Annie, who was being chased about the room by Josiah. Clasping the mouse-filled grocery sack, he had gleefully bumped Annie's leg with it.

And on this note the family party dispersed, Mrs. Sutton to deal with Josiah upstairs and Dr. Sutton to finish the task at hand. Eager to check the other traps, he called for Teresa, who had more empty grocery sacks bulging out of her pockets, to follow him.

Four out of the six traps had moved a significant distance, which caused Dr. Sutton much more headache than he had time for. Mrs. Sutton, ever resourceful and full of good ideas, suggested that he tie a piece of string to each trap. A portion of the string could then be pinned to its exact spot. Dr. Sutton would place it by the weight of the ceiling panel, which would cleverly close down upon it. Thus was solved the problem of traveling, dying mice.

The one downside of it was that no one could forget the presence of the traps and their mortal purpose. The remaining pieces of string hung down visibly throughout the basement ceiling. Voted the most unpleasant sight of the month was the vision of the dancing, dangling mousetrap strings that visibly spoke of a successful catch.

And that was how Dr. Sutton began to go fishing for mice. Never before had there been as successful a fisherman as he. Only a couple weeks of fishing were needed before the mice problem had almost vanished. And only a couple weeks did Allison and Bessie need to endure waking up to strings wriggling in the air.

Chapter 5

Sledding Expedition

WHEN THE GIRLS woke up one chilly morning during Christmas vacation, to their delight they found the window well filled with white, powdery snow. With uncontained excitement, they raced up the stairs and looked out the living room windows to find their very own winter wonderland. The rest of the household shared their enthusiasm. All appropriate gear was shoved and stuffed onto the various limbs of each Sutton child, with the exception of Baron, and they were on their way to scour their surroundings for the best sledding hill.

The only barrier that separated the Sutton backyard from the neighboring cow pasture was a barbed-wire fence. It had been weeks since a herd of cows had pastured there, so there was no concern that the children would be bothered by them. While there were no qualms about entering the pasture that lay behind their house, climbing over the red gate in order to enter that pasture was not without its challenges. The snowsuits that engulfed each warm body encumbered their efforts to mount the gate with every possible difficulty. By the time Allison, Bessie, and Teresa, who were the first to mount the gate successfully, landed safely on the opposite side of the fence line, they were in no humor to assist their remaining two siblings, who looked pleadingly from the other side.

Despite her own exhaustion, Bessie pulled down her scarf and said brightly, "Don't worry. We'll help you."

Josiah had managed to pull himself halfway up the gate, but his slippery boots limited any further progress.

Bessie's attempt to help Josiah, though brave in spirit, was that only. It came as no surprise to Allison that alone Bessie would not be able to bring over the other two. Bessie always was willing but not always able, while Allison was the opposite.

"I think one of us will have to get back on the other side and hoist them over," Bessie concluded.

In response Allison scaled the gate and leapt back down on their side of the fence. It didn't take much to boost Josiah over the top, and though no one caught him on the other side, with the combination of his winter apparel and the snowy landing, he stood up from his fall without complaint. But the amount of complaining done by Annie, the last member to be brought to the other side, was more than her siblings could tolerate. Crippled by fear, Annie would in no way make any attempt to climb higher than the first rung of the gate.

Trembling violently, she refused to be hoisted like her brother had been.

While Bessie continued to speak encouraging words from the other side of the fence, Allison grew impatient. Her toes were already going numb with cold, and they had not even begun sledding.

"Annie," Allison tried to explain, "the gate doesn't open because the snow is too high, so the only way you can reach the other side is to let us help you climb the gate."

Annie stubbornly shook her head and in desperation wedged herself between two middle rungs of the gate.

Allison seized this desperate measure and applied the pressure needed to get her sister through. With little struggle, Allison managed to thrust the lower part of Annie's body through to the other side. But this choice of pushing Annie's legs and middle was unfortunate, because, being yet little, the largest portion of Annie's body was her head. Within moments, every part of Annie, save her head, had triumphantly made it to the other side. But, sensing that her head would in no way follow the rest of her body, Annie began to shriek. Allison, having applied all the pressure she dared, gave up on the hope of passing Annie between the gate rungs and quickly reeled her back through. Shaking violently from sobbing, Annie marched back toward the house.

"Yes!" Josiah shouted as he watched the pathetic retreating figure.

"Josiah, that's not nice," Bessie said.

Allison stole a glance at Bessie. Bessie had really meant it.

Moving onward without much thought to their recent loss, save Bessie, the rest of the children began searching for a hill. Even before any attempts had been made to sled down a hill, Josiah hinted that his legs hurt.

"Could you carry me?" Josiah asked Allison.

Allison, who had most of the carrying responsibilities, quickly had Josiah on her back as they continued the search. They spotted a steep hill a short distance off and headed for it. By the time they reached the hill, which had not seemed far away at first, more than one of the children began suffering from exhaustion.

"It's going to be worth it," Allison promised. From the top, the hill looked perfect. The slope had just the right amount of angle, and the bottom was free of objects that would hinder the happy sledded flight as it finished off.

Allison assumed the job of being the first down the hill. Eagerly she settled into the sled that she had specially chosen from among the variety of sleds they had dragged along. Each sled had its own quirks. This one was only slightly broken, with a barely perceivable crack running through its side. Holding their breaths, the children watched their older sister prepare for takeoff. After taking a running start, she launched herself and her sled down the hill in the seated position. Without a word, the children watched the daring figure with shrinking hearts. From all appearances it had looked like the hill was as smooth as icing on a cake. Yet never before had the children received such a vivid lesson as they did that day of the well-known saying "appearances can be deceiving." To say that Allison did not glide down the hill smoothly was a great understatement. She did not sled down the hill—she bounced down. The vertical height she achieved with every bounce was amazing. And just as the sled never remained in contact with the ground for very long, neither did her bottom remain in contact with the sled. The ride was completed in a matter of seconds.

The remaining children at the top of the hill quickly grabbed their assigned sleds and ran down the hill after her. Nobody wanted to sled down. After witnessing such a flight, none could wish the same on themselves. They felt even better about their decision as they came upon Allison, writhing on the snow, her hands clamped in agony to the lowest region of her back.

Bessie immediately fell down beside her sister and asked, "Are you okay?"

Allison, who did not feel that a verbal response was necessary, merely picked up her sled and trudged off in the direction of another hill not too far off. The silence of the motley crew was soon broken by Josiah, who began mentioning his legs again. Allison bent down and offered her back. Gratefully, he boarded.

By the time they reached the next hill, their hopes again had risen, and Allison unselfishly suggested that Teresa try out the hill first this time. Teresa, prone to wild behavior, flung her body down the hill before any counsel was given and without further consideration on her part. The sled looked as if it had been tailor-made for Teresa's height and width. In toboggan-like fashion her body flew down the hill, whose steepness far outshone the incline of the previous hill. It was too late when the older children realized there was absolutely no runoff area. Where the first hill ended, another immediately began. Anxiously, the spectators hoped that Teresa, who was by now speeding at an alarming rate, would merely shoot up the next hill. But it was not so. While the front of Teresa's sled rammed into the crevice between the bottoms of both hills, the remaining portion of the sled, along with Teresa, continued forward. And so the children learned the second vivid lesson of the day—the definition of inertia.

For Teresa, the time for the catapulting had come. Ushered forth with the highest force of speed, Teresa's body remained plastered to the sled as it flung her into the next hill. So fast was she flung and with such energy, that while her body sunk into the hill, her sled fell empty to the ground. Still on top of the hill, the alarmed children, who had witnessed the magnificent event, stumbled and raced down the hill to aid their sister, implanted in the hill. After plying her out, they were greeted by the stunned face of Teresa. Only in Josiah's face shone admiration and respect.

With great excitement Josiah suggested they should name the hill "Dead Man's Run."

And so it was called from that day forth.

For the second time that day, Bessie fell beside one of her sisters and asked the inevitable, "Are you okay?"

As Allison had done before her, Teresa did not respond with an answer. After picking up her sled, she headed tearfully toward the house. The rest of the children followed, and no one said much. When all the coats, hats, mittens, scarves, and snowpants had been flung randomly on the mud room floor, they sat down to cups of steaming hot chocolate and sipped in silence.

Chapter 6

Sunflower Seeds

AFTER THE EXHAUSTING morning, and after having her stomach warmed with the therapeutic hot chocolate, Allison felt the need to relax in her room. They all did. Without a word, the sledding party dispersed.

Entering into the comfort of her own room, Allison let out a sigh. As she passed by the snow-filled window well, she noticed a flicker of movement. She moved toward the window, and upon closer inspection, noticed tiny tunnels that had been burrowed in the snow-covered leaves. Never fully able to appreciate a wonderful discovery by herself, she quickly went in search for Bessie.

She found Bessie washing up the hot chocolate mugs.

"Quick, I need to show you something," said Allison as she waited for Bessie to drop what she was doing and follow her.

"Let me just finish up these last two cups," Bessie said in a voice that hinted of martyrdom.

In due time Allison had Bessie's nose plastered against the window well, admiring the little tunnels that went this and that way alongside the window.

"It reminds me of the unit study we did on prairie dogs in fourth grade," Allison said. She reflected fondly on how the cute creatures made various tunnels leading to endless rooms, each having an important purpose of their own. Later their teacher had them design and draw their own prairie dog colony with as many tunnels and rooms as they wished.

"What do you think made it?" Bessie asked hesitantly.

"Maybe it's a mouse," Allison said. "It was lucky not to make its way into our house. Not with dad on the job."

"Yeah," Bessie said, glad for the mouse.

They observed for a few moments more, and then detected some shifting in the snowy leaves. Crumbles of leaves and snow were being pushed aside as a little, brown, fuzzy ball emerged.

"I'm sorry, but that is *not* a mouse!" Bessie said, scrunching up her nose in disgust.

"It's a mouse with a major nose problem," Allison joked, agreeing that, though mouse-like, its nose was much too long to be a mouse.

"I almost said, 'oh, it's so cute,' but it is really ugly," Bessie said.

Allison reflected on the creature's unfortunate nose, and somehow it became more endearing to her because of it.

"But it belongs to us, and it is living in our window well," Allison said with feeling.

"It's funny how we are grossed out by mice in our house, but we can be excited to have this little guy. One windowpane can sure make all the difference," said Bessie.

Both girls were surprised that the little mouse-like creature did not disturb them. They were not sure if this was because it wasn't a mouse, or because the critter was outside, or because they could see it face-to-face, unlike the creatures concealed in the ceilings. Maybe it was for all of the reasons.

"What do you think it is?" asked Bessie, feeling sorry for the creature with the misshapen nose.

While Bessie continued to watch the thing at its busy work of burrowing and snuffling, Allison disappeared a moment and then returned with their *Wild Animal Nature Guide.*

"I'll figure out what it is," she said, flipping through the pages. "Oh, here it is! It's a shrew."

"Well, it is better than a snake," said Bessie, turning to look at the page Allison held up triumphantly.

"A lot better!" said Allison. "If you ask me, this is getting fairly close to having a pet. The window well is the perfect cage, isn't it?"

"You know, prairie dogs live in big families. I wonder if this is the only one," she mused.

"Yeah, I wonder," Bessie said, scanning her eyes in all the possible spots where another shrew could be hiding in the window well.

"We could feed it. We could sprinkle nuts and seeds on top of the snow," said Allison, joining Bessie at the window.

"How do you know it eats nuts and seeds?" asked Bessie.

"That's what mice eat," answered Allison confidently. Then she went upstairs to hunt for some seeds.

Fearing that her mother would not be keen on the idea of feeding the shrew in the window well, Allison decided to search out the seeds and nuts on her own. All attempts of discovering seeds without asking anyone failed, and she began to brainstorm about creative ways to ask for seeds without giving away the real reason behind it. Loving to bake, she scoured through all different recipes that might call for seeds. But the only ones she found either had the word "healthy" in it or had a name like "Oat & Prune Muffins with Nuts." The names alone made her insides rumble. Leaving the kitchen dejected and defeated, she suddenly had an idea.

Hurrying to Teresa's room, she burst in. At first she didn't see her sister.

Hidden beneath a glorious fort, in Teresa's estimation, made out of bed sheets and tablecloths, Teresa remained concealed during the entire conversation.

"Do you still have any of those sunflower seeds you got a while ago?" Allison asked.

"Yes," answered Teresa guardedly.

"Could I have some of them?"

"Why?" Teresa was excited to think that she had something her older sister wanted.

"Because. I only want a handful," pleaded Allison. She heard a slight rustle from the middle of the fort and then detected movement from beneath a white-and-blue checkered table linen.

"They are in my 'special' drawer," came Teresa's voice.

Taking this as permission, Allison went over to the drawer Teresa called her "special" drawer. Inhaling as deeply as she could, she held her breath and pulled open the drawer, hoping to find the sunflower seeds quickly. Teresa's drawer stank. And it was no wonder, because the items Teresa deemed worthy as special enough to make it into her "special" drawer were an odd assortment. The space in the small cubicle was filled with small animal bones and many teeth, both animal and human. Many molars of different species were scattered throughout, including one that came from her own mouth. Besides teeth, there were a couple of small skulls and a piece of an antler. An old Cubs ticket from when Dr. Sutton took her and Josiah to a Cubs game the previous year lay safe in a clear sandwich baggy. Apart from a few other odds and ends, the only other thing was the packet of sunflower seeds that Dr. Sutton had bought her at the Cubs game.

"Only a few," warned Teresa, as she peeped one eye through an opening between two sheets, to make sure Allison would not abuse the definition of "a few."

Grabbing a handful, Allison said a hurried thanks and went off to feed her new pet.

Feeding the shrew was a nice thought. But the sunflower seeds that she had carefully sprinkled on top of the snow-covered window well remained there until spring came. It was another disappointment. As the snow disappeared, the shrew did as well. In the end, its absence was not a sorry one, and, subconsciously, Allison began hoping for the arrival of the next window well creature.

Chapter 7

Hello

BARNEY AND CLYDE arrived at the Suttons' rental house on a beautiful spring morning. No one knew how long they had waited on the porch to be discovered. Scarcely believing their eyes, the Sutton children would have rushed out to them with open arms if it weren't for Dr. Sutton, who investigated the situation first. Anxiously, all six children peered out the window as they watched their father make his acquaintance with the two newcomers.

They both had identification tags that listed the same phone number, and each had the wearer's name printed on it. Declaring the two as safe, Dr. Sutton went inside to make the necessary phone call while the children quickly made themselves two new friends.

Two dogs couldn't be more different. Barney had been ill-named, at least in Allison's estimation. Standing tall on long, graceful legs, he appeared stately and prince-like. The only thing about him that was not so elegant was his German shepherd coat, which was falling out in clumps. Clyde, on the other hand, hoisted himself about on four very short legs. It was a marvel that he could be Barney's traveling companion and could keep up with him. Two overly large floppy ears hung very low to the ground, as did his tongue. He would have been the most winning of the two were it not for the perpetual clueless look on his face. It spoke of fair-weather friend-ness. In contrast, Barney's somber and serious eyes silently spoke of faithfulness to the death.

"The owner didn't seem too surprised or concerned, as long as we didn't have a problem with them being on the property," said Dr. Sutton as he rejoined the children outside.

The children were enjoying their new friends immensely. While Allison, Teresa, and Josiah petted Clyde, Bessie and Annie gave their attention to Barney.

"Too bad they have owners already," whispered Allison, though loud enough for Teresa and Josiah to hear.

"Yeah," they both said in agreement.

"Apparently they live just below us in the 'holler,' as he called it. And his farm is alongside the 'crick,'" said Dr. Sutton as he massaged Barney's ears.

"Can they hang around our house if we don't bring them inside, Dad?" asked Teresa.

"I suppose if they don't cause a problem, I don't see any reason for running them off. He said they are always good about going back home when they get hungry," said Dr. Sutton, swishing his hands on his lap to rid them of dog hair.

Annie swatted at the dog hair that speckled the air. Dr. Sutton prepared to go back inside to get ready for work. With his hand on the front doorknob, he paused and looked back at the endearing scene on the porch, silently hoping that one day they could have a family dog. He smiled. He understood. He laughed. Closing the front door behind him, he wondered who looked more happy, the children or the dogs.

By this time, Clyde had lain back against Allison's leg, offering his belly for scratching. Barney, on the other hand, stayed seated in regal manner, as Bessie and Annie worked intently on helping him shed his coat. It was a tempting activity that was hard to quit once started, for his hair fell out in alluring clumps.

"If you look close enough," Bessie instructed, "you can tell which clumps are ripe for plucking."

To Clyde's chagrin, all the children wished to participate in the "plucking" process. Before too long, Barney had endured enough, and after leaving the porch, he sniffed his way around the Sutton home. Everyone except Allison, who decided to return to Clyde, followed Barney while he made his rounds.

Holding Baron, Mrs. Sutton glanced out the living room window onto the front porch. There she saw Allison dreamily stroking an oddly proportioned dog and numerous clumps of hair blowing across the planked flooring. The other children were gathered around an unattractive dog who looked like his coat had growth issues and who was presently making a poop deposit in her bed of flowers. Baron let out a tremendous squeal and panted like a dog.

In the end, as long as all dog dumps were taken care of, it seemed that both Mrs. Sutton and the rest of the family would be able to enjoy a time of peace from the ever-persistent conversation of having a dog. The children could enjoy Barney and Clyde's frequent visits, and Mrs. Sutton could find respite from the never-too-far-off question of getting a dog. It seemed too good to be true, and, all too soon, they were to find out that it in fact was.

Chapter 8

Good-Bye

THE ONLY PERSON who was not served well by the arrangement was Allison. The presence of the dogs only served to magnify her longing. She wanted to *own* a dog, a dog of her very own. Anything of her very own would have been better than dogs that belonged to someone else. Anything, that is, except goldfish. They didn't count.

It was Bessie who made the next window well discovery. While stirring a batch of brownies shortly after breakfast one morning, Allison heard Bessie's familiar gait up the basement steps. She noticed there was a little more pep in her than usual.

"Quick, come see what is in the window well now," huffed Bessie as she waited on the top step of the stairs.

Leaving the whisk inside the bowl full of brownie batter, Allison fumbled down the steps with wild anticipation.

When they reached their room, they stopped—noses only inches away from the window glass—face-to-face with a baby bunny.

"It's a *baby* bunny!" Allison said, stating the obvious.

Just as quickly as they had gone downstairs, they flew back upstairs, out the door, and over to the window well.

Getting down on their stomachs, they peered over the edge. A tiny bunny sat huddled, pressed against the windowpane, its belly moving in and out at a rapid rate.

"It's so tiny," said Bessie, as she watched her older sister slowly extend her hands and carefully cup the little pet in her hands.

It hadn't made any move to escape the approaching hands, although it did start to wriggle as soon as Allison began lifting it out of the well.

"I can feel its heart beating really fast, the poor thing," said Allison, marveling at how warm and soft it was.

"Do you think it fell in on accident?" asked Bessie, as she patiently waited her turn to hold it.

"Yes, and I'm sure that is why it was so scared when we found it," said Allison. "I'm sure it is too little to eat carrots." That was the first food item that came to mind.

"It probably still drinks milk," said Bessie.

"Here," Allison said, slowly placing the trembling bunny into Bessie's eager hands. "You hold it while I go and try to find out how we can feed it some milk."

She said "poor thing" one more time before making her way briskly back to the house with a new sense of purpose and importance. Beyond the joy of suddenly becoming a mother, she couldn't wait to be the news bearer of the latest addition to the Sutton family.

As she opened the door, Teresa and Josiah whisked by screaming, both wearing bandanas over their faces, holding plastic guns, and straddling brooms.

Allison cried to them, "We just found a bunny. Bessie is holding it outside, and I am going to try to find it some milk."

Teresa and Josiah immediately dropped their guns and broomsticks and, with their faces still partially hidden by bandanas, scooted out the door with no need for further explanation.

After giving a frenzied look, Allison finally found her mom and dad both downstairs in the laundry room, examining a wet spot in the drywall, which someone had reported earlier that morning.

"We just found a lost baby bunny. It's all alone and doesn't have anything to eat. I'm going to give it some milk but don't know the best way to go about it." Allison reported this in rapid succession.

While continuing to examine something on the wall, Dr. Sutton said, "It would be a lot better if you just left the bunny alone. I'm sure the mother is nearby. It has a better chance of surviving with its own mom than with you."

The truth was sad to hear.

"But what if it is really lost?" Allison asked as a sad, sick feeling welled up in her stomach.

"Why don't you try leaving it alone in the yard a little while and wait to see if it hops off on its own? It would be much better off with its mom," Dr. Sutton repeated.

"Can I watch it from a hidden place?" asked Allison, feeling crushed.

Dr. Sutton turned around to face his daughter and saw that her face was drawn in sadness.

"You can stand to leave it alone for an hour. If it does not find its mom, it will not be far from our house, and you can try to find it then. But hope that it finds its mom. It would be for the bunny's best."

Allison did not like thinking that she did not want the best for the bunny. She was certain that *she* was what was best. Dr. Sutton's word being final, with a heavy heart Allison related the information to Bessie. Softly, they placed the bunny in the dewy grass a little distance from the window well.

"Don't you think we should set it on the side of the house where there is no window well, so it doesn't fall in again?" asked Bessie.

"Yeah, I thought of that, but if it falls in again, that means we can keep it for sure."

Bessie remained quiet. She hadn't thought of that. It took all their willpower to leave the small creature to fend for itself in the wilderness of their yard. But leave it they must, and so they did.

As they closed the front door behind them, Bessie said, "Let's get the milk ready for it while we wait."

"How do you know we will find it when the one hour wait is up?" asked Allison painfully. Allison knew that the real reason she asked was to simply hear the calm reassurance her sister was always ready to give.

"Well, I don't know if we'll find it, but we can be all ready for it if we do," Bessie replied, smiling.

Allison loved her sister.

"So how should we feed it the milk? Any ideas?" Allison asked, beginning to open various kitchen cabinets at random.

Bessie joined in the search, and when Mrs. Sutton came up from the basement ten minutes later, they questioned her.

Without a second thought, Mrs. Sutton pulled open a drawer they had missed. It was where she kept their medicine.

"Why don't you try this?" Mrs. Sutton said, handing Allison a medicine dropper.

"Perfect!" Allison said.

"Yeah!" Bessie added.

As Bessie got out the milk, Allison looked at the retreating figure of her mother, who had gone back downstairs, and she thought, *There has never been a more resourceful woman. She is very well-read.*

Allison often found herself saying such things in her head. While Teresa liked to play that she was broadcasting a Cubs game, Allison enjoyed her private broadcast on life.

By the time the medicine dropper and milk were out and ready to go, Allison noted that it had only been fifteen minutes. Forty-five minutes to go.

"Let's go downstairs and play a game. It'll pass the time quicker," Allison said.

In the midst of a game of two-handed Pinochle, from the depths of the basement the girls heard the phone ring. It had only been twenty-seven minutes, and trying to discover who had called seemed like another perfect opportunity to divert their attention from the unbearable wait. They skipped up the stairs, Allison taking them two at a time.

The phone hung directly beside the door that led to the basement. So, if the basement door was closed, it was the perfect position to listen in on a call. It was closed. From the tone of Mrs. Sutton's voice they could tell it was their dad. The conversation was mostly one-sided and concluded with Mrs. Sutton saying, "Okay . . . all right . . . yeah, I'll tell them. See you tonight. Love you, bye."

Both girls started at hearing the words "I'll tell them" and scurried back down the steps. They rounded the corner just as they heard the basement door open.

"Allison . . . Bessie? Could you come to the bottom of the stairs for a minute?" Mrs. Sutton shouted down.

Being that they were right around the corner, Allison motioned to Bessie to remain still for a moment before they appeared.

When Mrs. Sutton saw them she continued, "Dad doesn't want you going up near the end of the driveway today."

Noticing that Allison was about to object, she added, "Not even to look for the bunny."

And then, in a softer voice, she said, "I'm afraid it looks like the bunny didn't make it."

"Did Dad see it?" Allison forced herself to ask.

"It sounds like he did when he left for work."

"If only I had kept it safe with me," groaned Allison.

"Then you would have been disobeying Dad," Mrs. Sutton said. "You did exactly the right thing, and I am proud of you, even though it was hard, and even though it didn't turn out well."

"But it died!" Allison said.

"Dad did what he thought was best, and it is not his fault or your fault that it died."

Bessie looked at Allison and appeared sorrier for Allison's pain than for the bunny. Allison, doing what she always did to deal with pain, went for a walk.

Stepping outside, she smelled the new fragrances of spring and already felt able to think more clearly. Avoiding the supposed scene of the crime at the end of the driveway, she decided to stroll about in the pasture behind their house. Before she had swung herself partway over the fence, Clyde and Barney joined her. She was certain they mourned with her and, therefore, was comforted in her loss.

As she let her body drop to the ground on the side of the pasture, she let out a stifled scream, to which Barney and Clyde immediately responded with excited barks. Her feet had barely missed the source of disgust. In that instant the mystery of the bunny was solved. So much of the bunny was there that she couldn't fathom what more of it could be left at the end of the driveway. It may have been easier to see it in shreds and pieces. But no, what was left of this bunny had taken on a completely different appearance. It was in the regurgitated form. That much she could tell, and she didn't want to know any more.

Barney and Clyde proudly stood above it, wagging their tails in admiration and then, to Allison's horror, attempted a second go at it. Allison shot back over the fence with more speed and agility than she had ever done, fleeing only inches ahead of the dogs, which had excitedly left their meals to chase after Allison. Imagining their mouths, which just moments before had touched the bunny, touching her, gave her an extra boost of energy to fling herself into the house and shut the door before the disappointed twosome stepped up onto the porch.

From that day forward Barney and Clyde were shunned, and to the relief of the Sutton family, their visits soon ceased altogether.

Chapter 9

Look What the Storm Rolled In

THE DAYS SLIPPED into weeks, and the weeks into months, and still the window well remained vacant. Despair crept in, and Allison abandoned her routine of looking out the window well and into the starry country sky above.

The week had been hot. Allison could not remember the last time it rained, and the thirsty pastures looked scorched. Mrs. Sutton was always watering her flowers. Even they, with all of Mrs. Sutton's extra tender care, were wilting. The sprinkler, which had been a great source of entertainment in the earlier summer months, had lost its grandeur, and so, with the added factor of the heat, the Sutton children settled for inside activities.

One morning, as Dr. Sutton bent down to pick up his medical bag and stethoscope, he reported to the early risers of the family, who sat around the kitchen table eating their cereal, that a storm was predicted later on that day.

"It'll be nice not to have to water the flowers today," responded Mrs. Sutton as she placed another spoonful of mushy oatmeal into Baron's wide-open, expecting mouth.

Allison thought he looked like a bird. *His food certainly looks slightly digested*, she reflected, *exactly like the food the mother bird brings up for its young*. She soon left off her contemplation as the images her mind conjured up became too disturbing, especially when she was eating breakfast. Suddenly, her soggy Rice Chex had no more appeal. Setting down her spoon, she drank the bowl of milk only.

The morning passed as typical late-summer mornings passed for the Sutton household—quickly.

One could even question whether there was an actual "morning" at the Sutton house, because Mrs. Sutton served lunch earlier and earlier each passing day of summer. Bessie had kept a journal, which she had found in Mrs. Sutton's "giveaway" pile. (Mrs. Sutton tried to hide this pile from the general household. These unwanted items, if found by the children, were almost always redeemed as invaluable treasures. She did her best to declutter, but somehow little progress was ever made.) This journal, rescued by Bessie, was originally intended to document the progress of a vegetable garden. Always keen on paperwork, Bessie had decided to document their summer lunchtimes. In the first week of summer vacation at the beginning of June, lunch had been eaten at 12:30 p.m. Having journaled each lunchtime in July, Bessie, who was also keen on math, had found the median time for each lunch. It was reported to be 11:30. Now that they were well into August, Bessie declared that the latest time they'd eaten lunch was 11:00 a.m. Mrs. Sutton was always a mixture of slight amusement and slight annoyance during Bessie's daily update, which she gave during lunch.

Being confronted on a daily basis with Bessie's report caused Mrs. Sutton to ponder the reason for this progressively earlier lunch hour, which, she concluded, was merely psychological. No matter what time lunch was eaten, she could fancy herself halfway through the day. And making it halfway through the day was an accomplishment worthy of praise. "Morning" could be checked off her list. She kept her conclusions to herself.

According to Bessie's log, lunch on that particular day had begun at 10:50 a.m. (The earliest record had been 10:46 a.m.) About two hours later, when the rest of the Midwest would be at lunch, a darkened horizon began inching toward the Sutton home. Even though the kitchen was lined with windows, by four o'clock, Mrs. Sutton needed to turn on the lights to begin preparing dinner. The impending storm stirred up silly behavior in all the children. As the beloved sounds of the roar of a diesel truck and of gravel crunching underneath its tires were heard, heralding Dr. Sutton's homecoming, the first raindrops began to fall. The appreciation of the cozy comforts of home heightened in the hearts of each Sutton family member.

As they sat down to dinner, Bessie proudly announced, "We had lunch at 10:50 a.m. today. We almost beat the record."

Dr. Sutton raised his eyebrows in amusement. Mrs. Sutton refrained from comment as she busily cut grapes into tiny pieces for Baron. Then she sprinkled them about his highchair tray. He deceived most of his family into thinking that he was swallowing them. Having fisted them, he shoved the small bits into his mouth and chomped a few times. But he never actually swallowed. The rest of the family continued eating in excited silence, which was only interrupted by an occasional exclamation of awe at the strength of the thunder that rumbled even in their chests. Dinner was quickly cleared, so that everyone could gather in the living room and watch the storm.

"Country storms are so much better!" Bessie said confidently.

For the entirety of their lives, the Sutton children had witnessed only city storms, those storms you had to watch with your neck craned up at the sky above you. Myriads of houses surrounding their old home blocked any hope for a horizontal view of the sky. But here in the wide-open country of pastureland and rolling hills, where the eyes could soak in valley upon valley, meadow upon meadow, woodland upon woodland, the storm became altogether different from in the city. Magnificent in might, spectacular in splendor, and brilliant in boldness, one watched the life of the storm. No longer did you wait for a bolt of lightening, but you breathlessly took in a shower of them. No longer did you wait expectantly to find out when the storm would ease up and when it would heighten, but you helplessly watched it come and go as it pleased. No longer, as the storm raged, did you feel safe and peaceful in the confines of a sheltered neighborhood, but you and your family braved the storm all alone, worrying about the cows somewhere huddled in the pasture. These thoughts and many more raced through the minds of the Sutton spectators.

Their pastime was interrupted by Josiah. "Baron has something in his mouth!"

"His cheek is bulging!" Teresa said as she slid down beside Baron. She always needed to be at the scene of the action.

Mrs. Sutton, who was not far behind Teresa, immediately groped inside Baron's mouth to find what was making it so full. And that is when they discovered that Baron had not swallowed any of his grapes, but had secretly pocketed them in the cavity of his cheek.

"He's got the whole lot of them wedged in the right side of his mouth. You can't do that, Baron. You'll choke on them." Mrs. Sutton sighed, her heart still racing from the thought of him choking.

Baron complained as soon as his treasure was stolen from inside his mouth. He had enjoyed the flavor.

An hour passed, and the storm continued. An hour more, and Mrs. Sutton told the children to get ready for bed, and that once they were ready they could come back for more.

As hard as it was for the children to tear themselves away from what lay before their eyes, they obeyed without objection. All of the children slipped away obediently without any prodding. Having just witnessed the majestic glory of something so radiant, they were subdued in wonder.

While waiting her turn for the bathroom, Allison wandered into her bedroom. Heavy droplets of rain pelted against the window well pane. She closed her eyes and listened. There were few sounds she enjoyed more. Her eyes opened, and then she found herself approaching the window well.

Chapter 10

Oreo

A SHEET OF water slid down the windowpane, distorting an unknown object that lay on the other side. Breathlessly, Allison made out a small creature sitting on its hind legs. Gradually, in quiet suspense, she brought her face to the watery glass. Looking back at her was a kitten. Deep, black, sorrowful eyes stared at her, patiently waiting for something.

Not daring to move as she recovered from the shock, Allison observed its coat, which was completely white, all except for a scant ring of black that circled its belly and one of its eyes. The kitten slowly lifted one of its tiny paws and softly brushed it against the windowpane. It was as if it were asking to come in.

With heart beating wildly, Allison did all she could to calmly walk out of her room, fearing that any sudden movement would scare her kitten away.

Whizzing past the bathroom, she whispered ferociously toward her unsuspecting siblings, all of whom were brushing their teeth, "There's a kitten in the window well!"

Despite the endless warning of never running with something in your mouth, let alone a toothbrush, the three Sutton children who had heard dashed into the bedroom to verify the happy truth. By the time the three had reached the living room, Allison was already well into an excited discussion.

"Please, could we at least keep it in the garage during the storm?" asked Allison in the most pressing tone.

Dr. Sutton, who was reading a pamphlet on beekeeping, laid it on his lap and said, "For one, it would be unwise for anyone to go out into the storm right now. And for another, the cat has found a safe place for the night and, I would think, is fairly sheltered from the weather down in the window well."

Allison felt the hot, tingly rush that preceded tears and asked in a shaky voice, "Would you at least come and see it?" She paused and then cautiously added, "If it was a puppy, you would."

Dr. Sutton rose from his chair, saying, "If it was a puppy, I would bring it into the house."

Although this comment surprised no one, all the children responded with their usual "Dad!" and Mrs. Sutton with her usual "Honey!" They all knew he had not spoken in jest, but truthfully. Dr. Sutton disliked cats. He even went so far as to say that when they had enough land of their own to build a barn, not even then would he allow cats on the premises. Even his nurse and patients knew about this abhorrence to cats. In an attempt to tease him, his nurse one day hung a cat calendar in his office. Always brilliant in comebacks, each month as the new cat picture was revealed, Dr. Sutton would invent a story to go along with the cat picture. Needless to say, the story always ended in the death of the cat. In absolute loyalty, all of the Sutton children had taken on this passionate dislike. As can be imagined, Dr. and Mrs. Sutton were then surprised to find such a sudden interest in the feline species. So, for the love of his children and not of the forlorn kitten, Dr. Sutton got up from his chair and followed the chattering crowd down to the window well.

Gathering around the window well, the children kept silent, hoping that their father would have a reversal of opinion. But the damp, furry kitten, who had curled up in one of the corners of the window well, was unable to change Dr. Sutton's mind. There was no sign that he was moved by the sight of the pathetic creature in the window well.

"Looks quite comfortable to me," said Dr. Sutton.

"What about in the morning?" asked Bessie, who had jumped onto her bed.

"What about 'in the morning'?" asked Dr. Sutton as he began heading out the bedroom door.

"Could we feed it just a little something in the morning?" asked Allison, finding it hard to mouth the words. The corners of her lips felt heavy and ached as she continued to fight back tears.

Dr. Sutton said, this time more sensitively, "If it's still here in the morning, I suppose you could, but if we start feeding it, it will want to stay."

Allison didn't hear anything past "I suppose you could," and was already sprinting upstairs to ask her mother if she could have a little container to use for the kitten.

"What do you plan on feeding it, Allison?" asked Teresa, keeping close to Allison's heels.

"Milk," she said confidently. But then, realizing she hadn't given the question any thought at all, she turned to Mrs. Sutton. "Do you think that is a good idea?"

"Yes, I'm sure. We can see if it takes to it or not," replied Mrs. Sutton. She found a plastic container that had lost its lid long ago but had managed to exist among the other containers.

"I wanted to throw out this container long ago," she said, handing Allison the clear, shallow container.

It was the perfect size—not too big, not too wide, and not too high. Lovingly, Allison placed it beside the front door, so that it would be all ready to use tomorrow. Having double-checked that there was a gallon of milk in the fridge, she hurried back to her bedroom. Bessie had by this time sunk down into her bed, and Annie and Josiah were committed to staring at the window. They both stood on chairs with their noses smashed against the window. Allison and Teresa, who was still following her, joined them.

"When will it move?" asked Josiah.

"Hopefully not till morning. We'll feed it as soon as we wake up," said Allison, feeling motherly.

"W'as 'is name?" asked Annie, pointing at the kitten.

"That's a good question, Annie," Allison said animatedly as she walked to Annie's side.

Examining the kitten, she asked Annie if she had a good idea.

"W'as 'is name?" Annie asked again. "W'as 'is name?"

"I don't know, Annie." Allison began running through a list of possibilities in her mind. None seemed good enough to say aloud.

"It looks like an Oreo," Josiah said, "only backwards."

Observing the belt of black that wound about its middle, Allison agreed, and before she could get the words out, Bessie shouted, "We should call it Oreo!"

Not sure how to express his excitement, Josiah, placing both hands on the windowpane, looked at the kitten, cocked his head to one side, and shouted, "Hi, Oreo. I'm going to eat you!"

Pulling on Allison's sleeve, Annie asked, "W'as 'is name?"

"His name is Oreo," Allison said, satisfied.

"All right, time for bed!" said Mrs. Sutton as she came in to collect Josiah and Annie.

Helping Annie off the chair, she reproached them for standing on chairs, especially chairs that swiveled. Sitting on the edge of her bed, Allison let the moment sink in. This was the closest she had ever gotten to having a pet sleep at the end of her bed. She had read about it in books. Eyes wide with pleasure, she slowly slid to the top of her bed, where her thoughts never went beyond the next morning and the little plastic container that waited by the front door.

Chapter 11

Bittersweet

ALL IN THE house was silent. Outside, a bird sang. Never before had it sounded so sweet.

Scrambling to the edge of her bed, Allison peered into the window well. It was too wonderful to be true. With a soaring heart, she ran up the stairs three at a time to the front door. She unlocked the door and opened it as quietly as she could, by pulling up hard on the doorknob to lessen the door's weight on its old, squeaky hinge.

Once again her destination was the window well, where she drew her tiny kitten from the fathoms below.

"Oreo!" she cried in a faint whisper.

Cautiously she brought the kitten to the front porch. It squirmed in her arms and meowed.

At first, Allison thought it might want to be put down, but when she tried this, the kitten did not seem satisfied. Bending down, Allison scooped up the willing kitten. Immediately it meowed once more, only this time much more urgently.

Then Allison remembered the plastic container. Softly tucked underneath Allison's arms, Oreo made her first entrance into the Suttons' house. Working at a frantic pace, lest Oreo's cries should wake up anyone, Allison picked up the plastic container and put it on the counter. If she had stopped to think about it, she would have brought both the milk and the container outside, and poured it out there. But in her haste, she filled the container inside the house and then tried carrying it and the squirming kitten back outside.

With her first step, the milk sloshed over the edge and onto the kitchen floor. She would have to deal with that later, she thought, and took another step, this time much more warily. Only a drip or two slipped over the edge and rolled down the side. With the kitten growing more and more impatient, Allison concluded it was much too risky to continue any farther at such a slow pace, so she lifted the container to her lips and drank two big gulps. Satisfied with the result, she continued toward the door and tip-toed out, shutting the door softly behind her.

Setting down both precious loads of cargo, she watched with delight as Oreo began to investigate the white liquid. Bending her head over the container, she paused, stopping within an inch of the milk.

With a heart swelling with pride, Allison watched the little pink tongue, first hesitantly and then eagerly, lap up the milk. Allison did not know how long she watched, squatting beside Oreo. After some time, Oreo, apparently finished, lifted her head and began to explore the porch. Just about this time, someone opened the front door. It was Bessie.

Bringing her finger to her mouth and whispering "*Shhh,*" Allison nodded toward Oreo, who was now walking the perimeter of the porch.

"Did she drink anything?" Bessie asked quietly, joining Allison on the floor.

Allison nodded. Together they watched in joy.

"This is better than Christmas," Allison said.

Both were very still as Oreo turned to scrutinize them. Then the front door burst open. About to give another frustrated "*Shhh,*" Allison stopped herself just in time, seeing her father standing there with a look of displeasure on his face. She then noticed he had one sock on his foot and the other in his hand.

"Did you spill milk on the floor?" he asked without raising his voice, though not hiding his irritation.

Scrambling to her feet she humbly said, "Ohhh! Sorry, Dad!"

Dr. Sutton didn't move from the doorway as Allison made a movement to go in.

Still holding the sock, he continued, "I stepped right into it."

Truly sorry and growing more grieved by the second, she attempted a second go into the house. (Dr. Sutton always preferred action that demonstrated true remorse over a mouthful of empty excuses, which is why Allison offered him none.)

"I already cleaned it up," Dr. Sutton said as he turned to go back inside the house.

The worst of feelings never failed to rise in her stomach when she heard her dad say that he had already fixed the problems she created.

Just before he closed the door, Dr. Sutton looked back at his daughter's disappointed face and said, "Next time, just take care of things right away. The point isn't that you spilled the milk; it's that you did not take responsibility to deal with it."

She nodded, too ashamed to look up at her dad. As soon as she heard the door close, she silently sat down again on the porch, frustrated at her forgetfulness. Dr. Sutton was right to assume it was her and not Bessie who had spilled the milk. Allison talked big, but Bessie acted big. Her only consolation was that she had the best of intentions, but even that was like sand in her mouth. Upset that she had messed up a perfectly good morning, she turned her gaze back to Oreo.

One by one the Sutton children woke up and joined the excitement on the porch. Many games were invented that involved the playful kitten. They set up a system where each person had an allotted time alone with Oreo. This worked well until it came to Bessie's turn. In horror, Allison observed Bessie's eyes growing watery, red, and itchy.

"Can you watch Oreo for a second while I run in to get a tissue?" Bessie asked, setting the kitten in front of Teresa.

"I'll get you one," said Allison, scrambling to her feet.

Bessie smiled, looking kindly at Allison, and thanked her. Anyone else would have questioned Allison why, all of a sudden, she would do something so out of the ordinary like that. Not Bessie. She always thought the best of everyone and so was not surprised that Allison wished to do this kind deed for her.

Little did she know that Allison was desperate not to let her mother or father see what she guessed and feared were allergies. By the time she came back out with a handful of tissues, Bessie was rubbing her eyes and sniffling.

"Maybe you shouldn't touch your eyes," Allison suggested, a bit annoyed at how puffy Bessie's eyes looked.

A simple tissue did not help the situation, which grew worse by the minute. It was a nightmare. They had come so far. They were so close. The pet was within their grasp.

Then, as Bessie's turn drew to a close, she spoke the words Allison dreaded to hear, "Do you remember the time we spent the day at Jackie's house? And we played with her cats? I feel the same way as I did that day. Maybe I'm allergic or something." Bessie stood up. "I think I need to get a warm washcloth."

Stressed and upset, Allison said, "Well, don't act like you're allergic. I'll go get you a washcloth if you need it. If they see you, then we won't be able to keep Oreo."

This statement distressed Bessie, and once she received the washcloth, she tried to dab away all allergic appearances. As time went on, Allison felt that it was of absolute importance to distract Bessie from her ailments, which seemed to cripple her more with each passing moment. Bessie never had a high tolerance for pain. For once, Allison wished it were her and not Bessie who had the cat allergy.

She at least would have borne it so nobly that no one would notice. She had once read of Fjords, a breed of horse that was particularly known for its stoic nature. If she had been a horse, she would have been a Fjord.

They played with Oreo until finally the exhausted kitten happily closed her eyes and snuggled close to Teresa. Allison said that, now that they were all on the porch (including Baron, whom she'd sent Teresa to collect), maybe their parents could talk about Oreo, and maybe they could keep her. This beautiful thought caused great love and patience to well up in each sibling's heart for one another. Never before had they played so kindly. But soon the younger ones began getting thirsty, and Josiah went so far to suggest that he was hungry.

Still keen on the idea that her parents might get a chance to talk alone about Oreo, Allison jumped up and announced she would go get everyone a snack and a drink. Josiah was nominated to go with her to help carry things back out. With an air of suspense, they walked into the kitchen. As she stirred up a gallon of lemonade, she directed Josiah to gather five cups and five bowls. She would bring out the lemonade and granola bars. On her way out she noticed that her mom was on the phone in her bedroom and her dad was downstairs at his desk. This disappointing fact dampened her spirits, but she managed to mask her concern before her siblings.

The snack having been eaten, and with Oreo still sleeping, there was really little else to do outside. Everywhere beyond the porch was wet and muddy from the rainstorm the previous night. Annie hinted that she was ready to go inside. But Allison wasn't about to let anyone go, afraid they'd interrupt a private parental conversation that she did not even know existed. Never short on ideas, Allison suggested a game of duck-duck-goose, one of the few games they could all play. To make it more challenging, Allison, Bessie, and Teresa had to hop on one foot. This occupied them for a surprising length of time. During their amusement, Oreo only opened a heavy eyelid every now and then. At one point the game got fairly wild, all participants eager to contribute their own amount of ruckus, hoping to fully awaken the sleeping kitten. But Oreo slept on. As the game neared its closure, hinted by "the look" that Allison and Bessie gave each other whenever they sensed a game had been milked for all its worth, the front door opened.

A rush of giddy hope surged in the hearts of the three oldest Sutton children, and they pretended not to notice their father, who was just stepping out onto the porch. Putting forth even more love and laughter than they felt, Allison, Bessie, and Teresa fought to produce and display an affectionate atmosphere for their father to see, all in the hopes of softening his heart toward their desire to keep Oreo.

"Looks like you wore the kitten out," Dr. Sutton said, looking on the scene with a loving air.

Everyone smiled and nodded, not trusting their voices.

Dr. Sutton stood for a moment or two and then sat down on a porch chair. "Well," he began, "I tried calling a couple places about the cat, but nobody knew anything about it."

Breathless, they awaited the conclusion.

"Now, you know it is for a number of reasons we can't keep it." Dr. Sutton looked at Bessie, who braved a smile through the teary, reddened puffiness of her sweet face.

"I'm going to take it to the pound, where I'm sure it will find a good home. They say kittens get snatched up pretty quickly," he said gently.

No one said a word.

Dr. Sutton turned to go back inside. "I'll need someone to go with me to hold the kitten. We'll go as soon as we can get in the truck."

In utter shock, Allison was unable to feel anything. She was going to ask if they could have just a little bit longer with Oreo, but thought better of it. She'd rather bring Oreo in and get it over with. *I woke up thinking this would be the best day of my life*, Allison thought, too embarrassed to say so.

Everyone except Baron piled into the truck. Mrs. Sutton had sent a couple of old towels to lay on the lap of whoever held it. No one objected when Allison took hold of the kitten on the way to the pound. Bessie, who now felt free to blow her nose at will, was much too uncomfortable in her allergic state, and Teresa, Josiah, and Annie were all too young. So it was Allison who cradled and caressed Oreo during the whole solemn ride.

She wished she had been completely alone with Oreo, so she could express to it all that was bursting within her heart and stuck in her mouth. Settling for something less, she poured out her feelings to Oreo silently.

It was not far to the pound, and it seemed even shorter for Allison, who savored every moment by drinking in the sweet vision of the small kitten cuddled safely in her arms. Dr. Sutton did not say much on the way over. He was never one to offer conversation for conversation's sake. But his somber silence at this time somehow seemed to communicate his sympathy for her.

Josiah was first to spot and announce the building. He then immediately kissed Oreo on one ear and said, "Good-bye."

This unfeeling and abrupt farewell, while certainly disconcerting, made Allison feel good about the extent of her own personal anguish.

The very building spoke of gloom. It was old and unkempt, and they would have guessed it was abandoned if not for the few cars sprinkled throughout the parking lot. Teresa got to the door first and held it open for the rest of the family to file in. Immediately they were hit with a stench that hung in the hot, thick air. Multiple fans were running, but they accomplished nothing but to swirl the gagging wafts around and about.

Dr. Sutton spoke a few words to the woman at the front desk, who appeared to be expecting them. She looked friendly. Her curly red hair was streaked with white wisps and piled on top her head, while stubborn loose strands clung to the back of her neck, moist with perspiration. She smiled at Allison, who still clung to Oreo, and said what a cutie pie the kitten was.

Allison tried to smile, but it felt as if clay had hardened on her face as she tried to lift the corners of her mouth to form the smile. But they froze, and the only thing that moved were crinkles around her eyes.

"Well," said the woman as she walked over to Allison, "from the looks of it, this one will not stick around here long. The kittens go the fastest, mind you." She placed her hands on her knees as she bent to eye level with Oreo.

She motioned for the group to follow her to the nearest door. The whines, whimpers, and wails that had been muted gained their full volume as she opened the door. The heavy odor of animals filled their nostrils as their eyes took in the endless cages of cats and dogs.

It was a hard sight for anyone to see, but it was especially hard for those who had a natural love of animals and a compassionate heart for the outcasts of society.

She continued to lead the way past a couple empty cages. Then she paused in front of the last and told Allison she might put the kitten in it.

"Just this morning someone was inquiring if we had a kitten available," said the perspiring woman as she clicked the crate closed.

"Does she have a name?" she asked as they all stepped back and watched Oreo walk the perimeter of her new home.

"Her name's Oreo," Teresa said proudly, stuffing her hands into the pockets of her overalls.

"What a nice name. I'll have to pass that along to the people who come to adopt her."

Allison waited for the group to move away from the cage and back to the door through which they'd come. Then she bent down and stuck her fingers through the slots of the metal cage.

Her voice trembled and it ached to talk, but she managed to whisper, "I'm so sorry we couldn't keep you. You will have a wonderful home somewhere . . . just not with us."

She couldn't continue. She tore her eyes away from the kitten, who had pressed her body against the cage as if to feel Allison's fingers against her fur, and stole out of the room just as the door was closing on the last person.

The next thing Allison knew, they were back in the truck and on their way home. Two great tears rolled down her cheeks. She never took her eyes from the window, wanting no one to see.

"Who would have thought that our first pet would have been a cat?" Dr. Sutton said.

Allison felt somewhat pacified by this statement, but didn't say anything.

"I thought our first pet was the snake," Josiah said in Annie's face, from whom he hoped to get a reaction.

Annie, being more repulsed by Josiah's breath than the thought of a snake, plugged her nose.

"Oh, yeah, and then the shrew!" Teresa contributed.

"And then the rabbit!" added Bessie.

"I wonder what will fall into the window well next," said Dr. Sutton, smiling.

Allison did not join the conversation. This did not surprise Dr. Sutton, for he knew she would feel the recent ordeal the keenest.

The somber party returned home to a house filled with the aroma of blueberries, cinnamon, and nutmeg. Mrs. Sutton had set the table with small dessert plates and glass cups, which she filled with cold milk as soon as they came through the door.

Over a piece of blueberry buckle, each child took turns at giving their own reports and accounts of what had just transpired. All, that is, except Allison.

Waiting till everyone had had their fill of talk and cake, Mrs. Sutton announced that it was her turn to say something.

"Mr. Dawson called right after you left," she said, more to Dr. Sutton than to anyone else. "Apparently, he has sold the rental house, and we are to move out at the end of next month." Her voice sounded robotic.

Allison did not hear the words that followed but walked mechanically down to her bedroom. She did not care about the news. She did not care about anything.

She did not know how long she had sat on her bed, staring up at her window well, when she heard a soft knock on her door. Turning, she saw it was her dad and looked sadly at him.

He joined her in looking out of the window well. "That wasn't an easy thing to do, not even for me," he said roughly, and then added, "and I don't even like cats."

Allison smiled, and for the first time in a while it came easily.

"You know, now that we will be leaving here soon, we'll have to find someplace that will be all our own. A place where pets *are* allowed."

"Maybe we can get a dog?" Allison asked. (She always liked to err on the side of under-asking than over-asking.)

"A dog, cows, sheep, and maybe even horses," Dr. Sutton said.

They were both quiet.

"Well, I have some things I need to go take care of now, and maybe you can run up and see how you could help out your mom. That is always one of the best ways to cure sadness, in my opinion. Stop thinking about yourself, and start serving others."

With that, he left the room for his desk, where he immediately made a phone call.

Allison took two quick steps toward the door and then paused to look up once more at the window well. All sorts of creatures had come to her through the window well, and now it was all about to end. They would leave in just a matter of weeks. She wished there would be enough time for just one more pet to fall into her window well.

Moving day came and went, and nothing else was ever found in the window well. Although this was cause for sadness, there were new things and new places to look forward to. Allison did not yet know it, but the pets and creatures that lay in store for her at her new home would go far above and beyond the confines of her wishing window well.